The Jacqueline Wilson Diary 2009

Illustrated by Nick Sharratt

DOUBLEDAY

Join the FREE online

Jacqueline Wilson

☆ FAN CLUB ☆

Read Jacqueline's monthly diary, look up
tour info, receive fan club e-newsletters.

All this and more, including quizzes,
members' jokes, a fabulous message board
and loads of exclusive top offers

Visit www.jacquelinewilson.co.uk

for more info!

Here is
a photo
of me

This diary belongs to:

Name: Lucy Kate Alderton

Address: 203 upton lane
Widnes Cheshire England
WA8 9PB ✵

Phone number: 0151 424 2818
07792005817

E-mail address: lucy_al_a_pink
girls@hotmail.co.uk

My Family

I've always thought it would be wonderful to be part of a very large family. I used to love reading books about big families like *Little Women* and *What Katy Did*. I'd imagine what it would be like to have lots of sisters. I often write rather wistfully about sisters who are very close to each other, like Ruby and Garnet in *Double Act* and Pearl and Jodie in *My Sister Jodie*. I was an only child and I longed for a sister to play with. I used to pretend I had one. I'd mutter to this imaginary person as I played with my dolls and she'd talk back to me. Sometimes we'd even have arguments. I must have been a very weird little girl.

I had my daughter Emma when I was very young. She became closer to me than any sister, real or imaginary. When she was small we'd play together, making up stories and acting them out. We'd cut out paper dolls, crayon fairytale magic lands, and play we were Victorians. Emma was very crafty: she always had to be the lady of the house and I was the servant doing all the work!

She's grown up now and has her own house (but no servant). We're still very close and phone each other every day. So I've still got a very small family — but it's a very special one.

by Jacqueline Wilson

My Family

I'm the oldest of four. We go boy, girl, boy, girl and there's about a year and a half between each of us — all very neat and tidy! What with us and our friends our home was always teeming with children. You can play great games with four or more. A real favourite was inspired by a television programme called 'It's A Knockout!'. We'd build a complicated obstacle course in the back garden, using the swing and the slide, beer crates, planks, sacks, an old tyre and gigantic cardboard tubes that Dad would bring us home from work. Then we'd divide into two teams and run races, timing ourselves to the second. Another excellent game was 'Avalanche' where we'd pile the staircase with foam rubber mattresses used on camping holidays and attempt a perilous ascent (this could only be played when the parents weren't too near). 'Shipwreck' was good too: the settee was a life-raft and we surrounded it with a treacherous sea made from massive quantities of torn-up newspaper.

And when we were lucky enough to live in a house with our own playroom I remember turning it into a disco one day by covering the walls, windows and ceiling in tin foil decorations, making special tickets and charging all the children in the neighbourhood a penny entrance fee to come in and join us dancing to our 'Top of the Pops' albums. The one thing we four Sharratt children had in common was that we all liked a really good bop, and that still holds true today!

by Nick Sharratt

My Family

In my family there are _4_ of us:
Mum, Dad, me and my
little brother Daniel.

The person who makes me laugh the most is:
my Dad

I have _0_ pets:

my mum
is a good listener.

My Family Tree

My granny	My grandad	My granny	My grandad
My mum's mum	My mum's dad	My dad's mum	My dad's dad
Kath Polhill	David Polhill	Sylvia Alderton	John Alderton

My mum
Angela Polhill

My dad
John Alderton

Aunties and uncles
(my mum's brothers and sisters)
Alynne, UDavid, USteven

Aunties and uncles
(my dad's brothers and sisters)
A Sylvia, A Bebbie, A lorraine, A Karen.

My cousins
Amy, Mathew, Sophie, Kay, 3 Andrew.

My cousins
Sean, Michael, Chres, Josh, James, Craig, lewis 3 laurie.

Me
Lucy Alderton

My brothers

Daniel Alderton

My sisters

Quick Quiz

 1 What is Floss's nickname for her half brother? _Tiger_

 2 Who moves with her family to the Star Hotel? _elsa in "The bed and breakfast_

3 What does Tracy tell everyone her mum is? _A famous Actress_

 **4** Who is embarassed by her parents? _mandy in badgirls_

 5 Whose real name is Jayni? _lola Rose_

6 Where was April Showers found as a baby? _Dustbin_

7 Who hopes that Cam will become her foster mum? _Tracy beaker_

8 Who has a pet called Mabel? _Verity in the cat mummy_

9 Whose mum moves to Australia? _floss in Candyfloss_

10 Who lived at 38 Fassett Road as a child? _Jaqueline Wilson_

 is for questions

Answers on the last page

Birthdays

and important days
to remember

My Birthday —15th July

My mums Birthday — 5th October

My Dads Birthday — 12th October

My Daniels Birthday 8th March

My New Year's Resolutions

1 ....

2 ....

3 ....

4 ....

5 ....

The resolution I think I'll be able to keep all year ....
....
....

The resolution I'll probably break first
....
....
....

My Record of 2009

I am aged 13

My best friend is Jessica Geraghty
Chelsie Kenny.

I get £............... pocket money every week

My favourite book is cookie "Jaquieline Wilson"

My hobbies are Dancing, Acting & Singing

✦ My Predictions ✦ for 2019

I will live in ....
....
....

My best friend will be ....

....

My favourite food will be ....
....

I will work as ....
....

I will spend my money on ....
....
....

Keep this page and in ten years' time you can see how accurate your predictions were!

My Timetable

	Monday	Tuesday
9.00		
9.30		
10.00		
10.30		
11.00		
11.30		
12.00		
12.30		
1.00		
1.30		
2.00		
2.30		
3.00		
3.30		
Homework		

$$9 \overline{)30^36} \quad \begin{array}{c} 34 \end{array}$$

Fill in your lessons here —
and don't forget your
after-school clubs and practices

Wednesday	Thursday	Friday

Important Addresses and Phone Numbers

Name: ....

Address: ....

....

....

....

....

Phone Number: ....

E-mail: ....

Name: ....

Address: ....

....

....

....

....

Phone Number: ....

E-mail: ....

Name: ....

Address: ....

....

....

....

....

Phone Number: ....

E-mail: ....

☆   ☆   ☆   ☆   ☆

Name: ....

Address: ....

....

....

....

....

Phone Number: ....

E-mail: ....

Name: ....

Address: ....

....

....

....

....

Phone Number: ....

E-mail: ....

Name: ....

Address: ....

....

....

....

....

Phone Number: ....

E-mail: ....

Name: ....
Address: ....
....
....
....
....

Phone Number: ....
E-mail: ....

Name: ....
Address: ....
....
....
....
....

Phone Number: ....
E-mail: ....

Dec / January

Pearl

My sister Jodie is the best sister in the whole world. I love my mum and I love my dad — but I love Jodie most of all. I don't know what I'd do without her.

Monday 29

Tuesday 30

Wednesday 31

Party!

New years eve!

Thursday 1

Friday 2

Saturday 3/ Sunday 4

January

I thought I'd glide off like a swan, swoop-swoop, swirl-swirl, the epitome of atheletic grace.

Monday 5

Tuesday 6

Wednesday 7

Thursday 8

Friday 9

Saturday 10

Sunday 11

January

I'm never quite sure if I like Lisa or Angela the best, so it's only fair to take turns.

Lisa   Me   Angela

Monday 12

Tuesday 13

Wednesday 14

Thursday 15

Friday 16

Saturday 17

Sunday 18

January

Once she bit me on the nose by accident. She can be a very boisterous baby sister.

Monday 19

Tuesday 20

Wednesday 21

Thursday 22

Friday 23

Saturday 24

Sunday 25

Jan/February

Jayni

I love my mum. I love
my little brother Kenny,
though he's a royal pain at times. I used to
love my dad but he got so scary we had
to run away. We've got new names now.
I'm Lola Rose. It sounds so cool, doesn't it?

Monday 26

Tuesday 27

Wednesday 28

Thursday 29

Friday 30

Saturday 31/ Sunday 1

February

I love my dad. He sometimes takes me out for treats on Saturdays, just him and me. For my last birthday he took me all the way on the train to Paris.

Monday 2

Tuesday 3

Wednesday 4

Thursday 5

Friday 6

Saturday 7

Sunday 8

February

'I love you too,' I whisper,
and then I put the phone down.

Monday 9

Tuesday 10

Wednesday 11

Thursday 12

Friday 13

Saturday 14

Valentine's Day

Sunday 15

February

Never mind Elaine's inner child.
I am her outer child and it's mega-difficult to make
contact with her, even when I bawl my head off.

Monday 16

Tuesday 17

Wednesday 18

Thursday 19

Friday 20

Saturday 21

Sunday 22

Feb/March

Floss

I don't know what to do. My mum and my stepdad Steve and my baby brother Tiger are going to live in Australia. I want to go with them — but I want to stay with my dad too. I love my dad so much. I love his chip butties too!

Monday 23

Tuesday 24

Wednesday 25

Thursday 26

Friday 27

Saturday 28/ Sunday 1

March

As it was Marigold's thirty-third birthday I decided I'd draw her thirty-three most favourite things.

Monday 2

Tuesday 3

Wednesday 4

Thursday 5

Buy the new Jacqueline Wilson novel today!

Friday 6

Saturday 7

Sunday 8

Diaries are Boring x

March

I built her up into such a little Baby Wonder
that the kids in my class were drooling
and they all wanted to see the show
with me and this mega brilliant little brat.

Monday 9

Tuesday 10

Wednesday 11

Thursday 12

Friday 13

Saturday 14

Sunday 15

March

Half of me wanted to side with Mum. Half of me wanted to side with Dad. It was much easier for Radish. She just sided with me.

Monday 16

Tuesday 17

Wednesday 18

Thursday 19

Friday 20

Saturday 21

Sunday 22

Mother's Day

March

Mum got me all beautifully dressed up — though we both fell about laughing when I tried the black dress on because it came right down to my belly button.

Monday 23

Tuesday 24

Wednesday 25

Thursday 26

Friday 27

Saturday 28

Sunday 29

March/April

April

I dread it when anyone asks me about my family. I haven't got one. I must have had a mum, obviously, but she left me in a dustbin when I was a tiny baby. I don't have a clue who she is — but I'd give anything to find her.

Monday 30

Tuesday 31

Wednesday 1

Thursday 2

Friday 3

Saturday 4/Sunday 5

April

Loop after loop. Coil after coil. A snake!
An enormous brown snake, with a mean
head and a forked tongue flicking in and out.

Monday 6

Tuesday 7

Wednesday 8

Thursday 9

Friday 10

Good Friday

Saturday 11

Sunday 12

Easter Sunday

April

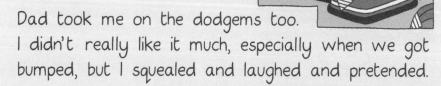

Dad took me on the dodgems too.
I didn't really like it much, especially when we got
bumped, but I squealed and laughed and pretended.

Monday 13

Tuesday 14

Wednesday 15

Thursday 16

Friday 17

Saturday 18

Sunday 19

April

Vincent is getting a back tooth and has turned into a human waterfall.

Monday 20

Tuesday 21

Wednesday 22

Thursday 23

Friday 24

Saturday 25

Sunday 26

April/May

Tracy

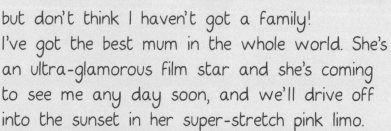

I might live in
a Children's Home
but don't think I haven't got a family!
I've got the best mum in the whole world. She's
an ultra-glamorous film star and she's coming
to see me any day soon, and we'll drive off
into the sunset in her super-stretch pink limo.

Monday 27

Tuesday 28

Wednesday 29

Thursday 30

Friday 1

Saturday 2/ Sunday 3

May

Poor little Cinderella Beaker had to stay at home and tackle all the chores.

Monday 4

Tuesday 5

Wednesday 6

Thursday 7

Friday 8

Saturday 9

Sunday 10

May

Pippa and Hank aren't my proper sister and brother. They're halves.
That sounds silly doesn't it. We've all got the same mum. Our mum. But I've got a different dad.

Monday 11

Tuesday 12

Wednesday 13

Thursday 14

Friday 15

Saturday 16

Sunday 17

May

I didn't know many of the songs but I've always been good at improvising. So I threw back my head and let it rip.

Monday 18

Tuesday 19

Wednesday 20

Thursday 21

Friday 22

Saturday 23

Sunday 24

May

The inspector really did take us out in a big police car. He wouldn't go very fast but he did put the siren on just for a second.

Monday 25

Tuesday 26

Wednesday 27

Thursday 28

Friday 29

Saturday 30

Sunday 31

June

Dolphin

I love my mum
Marigold so much.
She's the most magical mum in the whole world.
I think she looks beautiful, with her long red
hair and her amazing artistic tattoos, but my
sister Star hates our mum looking so unusual.

Monday 1

Tuesday 2

Wednesday 3

Thursday 4

Friday 5

Saturday 6/Sunday 7

June

Callum caught us and he turned me upside down and shoogled me until I felt sick.

Monday 8

Tuesday 9

Wednesday 10

Thursday 11

Friday 12

Saturday 13

Sunday 14

June

Rhiannon let me shake all her snowdomes and wind up her Cinderella musical box.

Monday 15

Tuesday 16

Wednesday 17

Thursday 18

Friday 19

Saturday 20

Sunday 21

Father's Day

June

I'd play games with the dummy and sometimes hug her. She felt exactly like my grandma in her corsets.

Monday 22

Tuesday 23

Wednesday 24

Thursday 25

Friday 26

Saturday 27

Sunday 28

June/July

Verity

I don't have a
mum. She died
when I was born.
But it's OK, I have a
lovely dad and Gran and Grandad.
I also have a dear old cat called Mabel.

Monday 29

Tuesday 30

Wednesday 1

Thursday 2

Friday 3

Saturday 4/ Sunday 5

July

I've done a bit of stamping
and screaming in my time.

Monday 6

Tuesday 7

Wednesday 8

Thursday 9

Friday 10

Saturday 11

Sunday 12

July

I could feel the baby's warm pink scalp, so small, so delicate. I decided I was going to love my new little brother no matter what.

Monday 13

Tuesday 14

Wednesday 15

Thursday 16

Friday 17

Saturday 18

Sunday 19

July

Sometimes I can see why Mum can't face food herself. Mopping up my baby brother would put anyone off their breakfast.

Monday 20

Tuesday 21

Wednesday 22

Thursday 23

Friday 24

Saturday 25

Sunday 26

July/August

Charlie

My mum Jo and I have a lot of fun together. I can generally get her to do what I want. It's easy-peasy, simple-pimple. So why is she getting so keen on this loser Mark and his weird little kid Robin?

Robin

Monday 27

Tuesday 28

Wednesday 29

Thursday 30

Friday 31

Saturday 1/ Sunday 2

August

Clive wasn't the only one
who was sick on the train going home.

Monday 3

Tuesday 4

Wednesday 5

Thursday 6

Friday 7

Saturday 8

Sunday 9

August

Vita and Maxi were half asleep, cuddled up like puppies, chocolate drool around their mouths.

Monday 10

Tuesday 11

Wednesday 12

Thursday 13

Friday 14

Saturday 15

Sunday 16

August

I was delighted at breakfast to see that Justine had a swollen nose and a sticking plaster.

Monday 17

Tuesday 18

Wednesday 19

Thursday 20

Friday 21

Saturday 22

Sunday 23

August

We shadow-sparred for a minute, miming kick boxing and kung fu.

Monday 24

Tuesday 25

Wednesday 26

Thursday 27

Friday 28

Saturday 29

Sunday 30

Aug/September

Ruby and Garnet

We're twins. We're
absolutely identical.
We live with our dad
and our gran. We still
miss our mum very, very much.
We don't ever want a stepmum. So clear off Rose!

Monday 31

Tuesday 1

Wednesday 2

Thursday 3

Friday 4

Saturday 5/ Sunday 6

September

He's really called Tim, but
Tiger suits him better.

Monday 7

Tuesday 8

Wednesday 9

Thursday 10

Friday 11

Saturday 12

Sunday 13

September

I use a wheelchair. It's electric and powerful so sometimes I can muck about chasing the other kids.

Monday 14

Tuesday 15

Wednesday 16

Thursday 17

Friday 18

Saturday 19

Sunday 20

September

One time she took my box of felt-tip pens and designed amazing tatoos for her arms and legs.

Monday 21

Tuesday 22

Wednesday 23

Thursday 24

Friday 25

Saturday 26

Sunday 27

Sept/October

Andy

I live one week with my mum and her boyfriend Bill the Baboon and his children Paula and Graham and Katie. I live the next week with my dad and his girlfriend Carrie and her twins Zen and Crystal. I wish I still lived with Mum and Dad — and my little rabbit Radish.

Monday 28

Tuesday 29

Wednesday 30

Thursday 1

Buy the new Jacqueline Wilson novel today!

Friday 2

Saturday 3/ Sunday 4

October

I shot up in the air again, so happy
I was bouncing up to the ceiling.

Monday 5

Tuesday 6

Wednesday 7

Thursday 8

Friday 9

Saturday 10

Sunday 11

October

Naomi's mum was stirring a bean stew. She had baby Nathan on her hip, and he was smacking his lips in anticipation.

Monday 12

Tuesday 13

Wednesday 14

Thursday 15

Friday 16

Saturday 17

Sunday 18

October

Mum told me stories about when
I was a very little girl. I told Mum stories about
what I plan to do when I am a big girl.

Monday 19

Tuesday 20

Wednesday 21

Thursday 22

Friday 23

Saturday 24

Sunday 25

Oct/November

Elsa

I tell jokes all the time to try to cheer us up. My mum doesn't laugh very much. My stepdad Mack tells me to quit the funny stuff. But my little sister Pippa loves my jokes and my baby brother Hank giggles at me too, especially when I tickle his tummy.

Monday 26

Tuesday 27

Wednesday 28

Thursday 29

Friday 30

Saturday 31/ Sunday 1

Halloween

November

The most magical comic
of all was *Girl*.

Monday 2

Tuesday 3

Wednesday 4

Thursday 5

Bonfire Night

Friday 6

Saturday 7

Sunday 8

November

Sometimes at night in bed I pretended I was adopted and that one day my real mum and dad would come and take me away. They'd be ever so young and hip and stylish.

Monday 9

Tuesday 10

Wednesday 11

Thursday 12

Friday 13

Saturday 14

Sunday 15

November

Mum made me try on loads of frocks but they all looked *awful*.

Monday 16

Tuesday 17

Wednesday 18

Thursday 19

Friday 20

Saturday 21

Sunday 22

November

I looked at my illustrated mum. I knew
she really did love me and Star. It didn't
matter if she was mad or bad.

Monday 23

Tuesday 24

Wednesday 25

Thursday 26

Friday 27

Saturday 28

Sunday 29

Nov/December

Dixie

We are the Diamond girls. There's my mum, Sue, and my three sisters, Martine, Jude (she's my favourite) and Rochelle. I'm Dixie. I was the youngest, but now my mum's going to have another baby — only this time she's sure it's going to be a boy.

Monday 30

Tuesday 1

Wednesday 2

Thursday 3

Friday 4

Saturday 5/ Sunday 6

December

Some stupid little kid had set a small herd of plastic dinosaurs to graze on the carpet.

Monday 7

Tuesday 8

Wednesday 9

Thursday 10

Friday 11

Saturday 12

Sunday 13

December

I chalked pictures - three
round blobs with stick arms
and smiles across their stomachs.

Mummy Daddy Me

Monday 14

Tuesday 15

Wednesday 16

Thursday 17

Friday 18

Saturday 19

Sunday 20

December

EEYORE! EEYORE!

I'm going to be acclaimed as a brilliant child star. I shall have the STAR part in a major production this Christmas.

Monday 21

Tuesday 22

Wednesday 23

Thursday 24

Friday 25

Christmas Day

Saturday 26

Boxing Day

Sunday 27

Dec / January

Dad let me take my time, circling the roundabouts so that I could see every single horse and see which one I liked best.

Monday 28

Tuesday 29

Wednesday 30

Thursday 31

New Year's Eve

Friday 1

New Year's Day

Saturday 2

Sunday 3

Important Dates to Remember for

....

....

....

....

....

....

....

....

....

....

....

....

....

....

....

....

....

....

....

....

....

Have you read all these wonderful books
by Jacqueline Wilson?

Published in Corgi Pups, for beginner readers:
THE DINOSAUR'S PACKED LUNCH
THE MONSTER STORY-TELLER

Published in Young Corgi, for newly confident readers:
LIZZIE ZIPMOUTH
SLEEPOVERS

Published in Doubleday/Corgi Yearling Books:
BAD GIRLS
THE BED & BREAKFAST STAR
BEST FRIENDS
BURIED ALIVE!
CANDYFLOSS
THE CAT MUMMY
CLEAN BREAK
CLIFFHANGER
THE DARE GAME
DOUBLE ACT
GLUBBSLYME
THE ILLUSTRATED MUM
JACKY DAYDREAM
LOLA ROSE
THE LOTTIE PROJECT
MIDNIGHT
THE MUM-MINDER
MY SISTER JODIE
SECRETS
STARRING TRACY BEAKER
THE STORY OF TRACY BEAKER
THE SUITCASE KID
VICKY ANGEL
THE WORRY WEBSITE

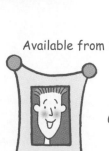

Available from Doubleday/Corgi Book, for older readers:
THE DIAMOND GIRLS
DUSTBIN BABY
GIRLS IN LOVE
GIRLS OUT LATE
GIRLS UNDER PRESSURE
GIRLS IN TEARS
LOVE LESSONS
KISS

THE JACQUELINE WILSON DIARY 2009
A DOUBLEDAY BOOK 978 0 385 61464 1

Published in Great Britain by Doubleday Books,
an imprint of Random House Children's Books

This edition published 2008

1 3 5 7 9 10 8 6 4 2

Text copyright © Jacqueline Wilson, 1991, 1992, 1993, 1994, 1995, 1996,
1997, 1998, 1999, 2000, 2001, 2002, 2003, 2004, 2005, 2006, 2007, 2008
Illustrations copyright © Nick Sharratt, 1991, 1992, 1993, 1994, 1995, 1996,
1997, 1998, 1999, 2000, 2001, 2002, 2003, 2004, 2005, 2006, 2007, 2008

The right of Jacqueline Wilson to be identified as the author of this work
has been asserted in accordance with the Copyright, Designs and Patents Act 1988.

Compiled by Harpreet Purewal

The Random House Group Limited makes every effort to ensure that the papers
used in its books are made from trees that have been legally sourced from
well-managed and credibly certified forests. Our paper procurement policy can
be found at: www.randomhouse.co.uk/paper.htm

RANDOM HOUSE CHILDREN'S BOOKS
61-63 Uxbridge Road, London W5 5SA

www.kidsatrandomhouse.co.uk

Addresses for companies within The Random House Group Limited
can be found at: www.randomhouse.co.uk/offices.htm

THE RANDOM HOUSE GROUP Limited Reg. No. 954009

A CIP catalogue record for this book is available from the British Library.

Printed and bound in Singapore

QUIZ ANSWERS

1. Tiger   2. Elsa in *The Bed and Breakfast Star*

3. A famous actress   4. Mandy in *Bad Girls* 5. Lola Rose

6. In a dustbin   7. Tracy Beaker   8. Verity in *The Cat Mummy*

9. Floss in *Candyfloss*   10. Jacqueline Wilson